Tokyo
Narita

Leilani
Gracetta

First paperback edition June 2020

Book cover design by Leilani Graceffa

ISBN 978-1-7350952-3-3 (Paperback)
ISBN 978-1-7350952-4-0 (Hardcover)
ISBN 978-1-7350952-5-7 (Ebook)

For more information, visit www.leilanigraceffa.com.

Discrimination: the unjust or prejudicial treatment of different categories of people or things, especially on the grounds of race, age, or sex.

For Christina, Charlie, Emily, all of the smiles familiar with the feeling of this story and whom this may concern.

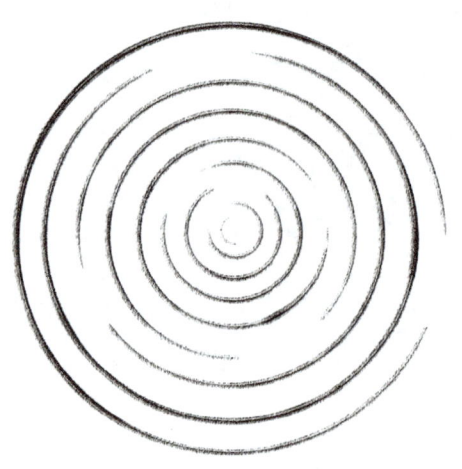

CHAPTER 1

I'm not trying to die, I don't want to die, but the bureaucracy chooses otherwise. If I don't keep moving, they will find me hiding in this range, not even considering extending my date. They'll execute me as quickly and ruthlessly as possible. But I'm not letting them do a damn thing to me, not anymore.

The light lines engraved into the rings' border walls are illuminating red. They are usually viridian; they know I'm on the loose. My turquoise hair and watercolored sleeve tattoos do not blend in with the falling snow up here, neither does my orange prison sweats and black tank top. If an officer spies me, I will be the dictator's mounted example of all of my people's eventual fate.

My keeper, Ivan Andrade, made me blow a fuse saying degrading shit to me, believing I wouldn't eventually attack him. Since he's the second most important person in Tokyo Narita, the dictator's aristocrat. He makes sure that is burnt into my mind. I blew a gaping hole through his chest with my powers. Even though I know damn well

Tokyo Narita

Dictator Victor might just serve me the death sentence for that—after all the times I've gotten into trouble. He gave me multiple chances to abide abuse, I will never fucking regret it. It's not my fault I'm left-handed! It never was.

He's so fucking spiteful and ignorant! His deaf and left-handed stepmother assassinated his father, the former dictator. That made him snap on left-handed and impaired people (or ciphers, as he loves to call us). So he decided to distribute a law, dividing us from the "normal" privileged right-handed citizens. Forcing all of us into concentration camps, having to endure lurid conditions and constant abuse.

"Eva?" I suddenly hear a voice behind me... a barely familiar voice, say with a concerned tone. "Where have you been?"

"Yeah, it's me," I reply, irked that it's most likely one of the people the dictator sent to find me. If only I still had most of my eyesight, I would be able to see and watch my back fully. I was nearly wholly blinded after getting some biochemical and gasoline mixture shit thrown in my face years ago. A grey fog clouds 90% of my vision, I can only see vivid colours and shadows. "Are you happy now?"

"I'm not one of them, Eva. It's me, Hunter."

"Hunter…" My best friend. I hadn't seen him since the last time the dictator granted me permission to be with Hunter for a day when we were kids. He grabs onto my hand, then pulls me into a firm embrace. Something I haven't felt since my betraying ass father turned me in to the dictator. "How'd you find me?" I ask, my voice breaking.

"I saw you hopping the borders, so I followed you."

"How did you follow me so fast?"

"I… have powers, like yours."

"What?" I'm confused. How is he not in an excluded cell, locked away from the general population like I am? This is especially so since he's a soldier in training, and he's around hundreds of people almost every day. Is it the privilege, or he hides it well, and they just don't know yet?

"I'll explain later..." He answers, hinting a bit of fear in his voice. He quickly drapes something over my head... it feels like a sweatshirt. A hoodie. "They're coming."

I scurry it on. The orange still screams for everybody to pay attention to me.

"COME ON!" As soon as we start to hear the roaring engines of military combat vehicles, he grabs onto my hand, and we bolt further into the mountain range. I have ominous nightmares and flashbacks of the many times officers and soldiers threw me into them and held me down. Whenever I screamed and fought back with the electric cuffs bounding my hands behind my back. Usually, when they needed to move me to another camp, they had to beat my ass every time.

We hide behind a large trunk of a tree away from the path. Hunter, being the eyes for both of us, watches as a group of soldiers, likely the ones with the black mechanical, armoured bodysuits and bioweapons, scatter from each other, in search of me. "You need to lose the pants."

"I know." I'll be running around in the snow without pants on, but if it means I'll be less noticeable, then fuck it. If we're lucky enough to stay out of sight long enough, they won't catch me by the tattoos on my legs. "How are we going to get out?"

"We can leave after it gets dark. I can sneak you into my apartment complex… and find you another pair of pants…"

"How many rings are we hopping?"

"23. Try to follow my energy."

"Okay." Since there's now a curfew, this should be easy since nobody, but soldiers are out patrolling the entry points. Using our powers, we start to dash up and down each wall, then rush kilometres through the dimly lit darkness to the next one, avoiding being close to the entry points. Every wall we dash up, I count, until we finally go over the 23rd one, then run to his apartment complex. We sneak in through the back door.

I have a lot to tell him, he has a lot to say to me.

"You go first." He says after we accidentally start talking at the same time.

"I went to prison, Hunter. My father turned me in and abandoned me. These officers threw me into multiple camps with soldiers that beat us, raped us, starved us, threw fucking chemicals in my face and fucking blinded me! And Dictator Dickhead doesn't do shit about it! He doesn't give a fuck. He claims that he cares for the divided population to you and the free and privileged people. It's a fucking lie! That motherfucker is evil, and he's hiding what he's doing. If I didn't have these tattoos, you'd see all of the scars I have. He assigned Ivan Andrade as my keeper, and I killed him. That's why they're after me now."

"Wait, Eva," He answers, sounding concerned, "What do you mean? What…?"

"He lied to you, he's been lying to everyone. That hand separation law that he uses to divide us, he's not taking care of us left-handed and impaired people like he says he is. He's shoving us into camps to let the officers and soldiers kill us. He favours right-handed and able-bodied people, and strips the rest of us of our identities and labels us as ciphers, with fucking numbers. And Ivan… kept talking shit to me, and I blew a hole into his fucking chest because I was fucking tired of it! He automatically opts everybody in to be a soldier to fuck people like me up."

"Shit…"

"I know it's a lot to process, Hunter. He tricked everybody into believing he's some kind of saint for dividing us. He's only doing it because his stepmother assassinated his father. And if you don't already know, the woman was left-handed and deaf."

"That is fucked up, Eva."

"Yeah, I know. But enough of that because I already hate talking about it." I rub my forehead. "You go."

Tokyo Narita

"I think I got my powers from you. I didn't have them until after we spent that day together, years ago. I had to teach myself how to use them, my dad found out about them, and he wanted me to keep them a secret. I didn't know where I got them from until an article said that you were the prime suspect in that massacre in a ring in East Narita, years later."

"That wasn't a massacre, it was a freak accident. He only called it that because he hates me, he won't give me a fucking break, and I'm a troublemaker in his eyes! Never gave me a fucking trial and started isolating me! My powers activated, and it let out some kind of wave of radiation and killed everybody around me. I couldn't see it. That was not my fault. But of course, he assumes everything when it comes to me because I'm a minority! And it's not just me, they're torturing and killing thousands of other people for things they can't control."

"I wish I'd known all of this before choosing not to opt-out."

"Don't opt-out, yet. I need you, and I need Cheyenne and Rholanda to help me."

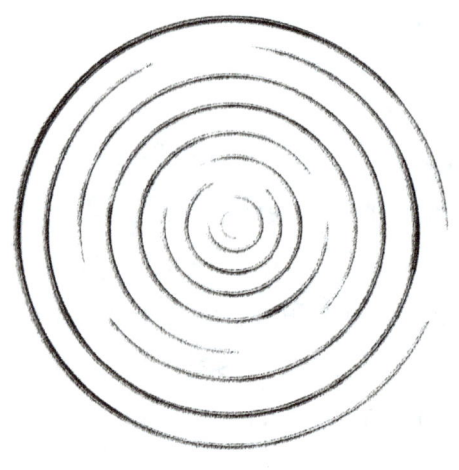

CHAPTER 2

I consider Rholanda my second mother. She took care of Hunter and I when we were babies, and she did my tattoos. The last time I've seen her was a few years ago when she finished my left sleeve tattoo. I wanted to tell her how I got all of my scars, but Ivan was there.

On a more serious note, she was the former aristocrat shortly for the current dictator and mostly his father. She quit and disappeared because she found out that the separation law was being processed, that was a secret at the time.

After Hunter finds me a pair of pants, I lay down in the backseat of his car, and we go to North Narita to see Rholanda and her daughter, Cheyenne.

"Rholanda, I got Eva."

"Hey, Eva." I hear from above.

"Who is that?"

"Cheyenne," Hunter replies. "She can't see you, Cheyenne. She lost her sight."

"How'd you lose your sight?"

"You can't see us at all?" Rholanda asks, waving in front of me.

"I can see your shadow, you're waving."

"How did that happen?"

"I wanted to tell you while I was getting my sleeve a few years ago, but my keeper was there…"

"Ivan Andrade, is your keeper?"

"He was." I chuckle. "I killed him, and the dictator sent his puppets to find me. I need help on that note."

"Okay, before you ask or tell me anything, would either of you like some of the food I just finished cooking for Cheyenne?"

My tastebuds have been deprived of even decent tasting food for so long... my eyes widen, and I answer with, "Yes!" the same time Hunter does.

Aside from my questions about Dictator Dickface and his self-centred bullshit, I've decided to hear more information from Rholanda and Cheyenne. About my parents, how my dad left my mom and decided to side with the dictator, why he turned me in, and other shit that I need to know.

"Your father is a very ungrateful man. He was embarrassed to have you, Eva. He wanted a son, and he insisted on secretly aborting you while your mother was pregnant with you. He wanted a reason to get rid of you."

I've always wondered why that bitch was always so cold and distant towards me but wasn't with Hunter. I watched him detach himself from mom and me, and I bet he despises me even more now since I'm considered a troublemaker. I have a burning feud with the dictator.

"Your mom, on the other hand," Cheyenne chimes in, "is my night training lieutenant on the base in East Narita. She's nice, but she's cold, and she does not let anybody, but me, in her office. She has pictures of you in there. Maybe that jackass doesn't care, but your mom does, and she misses you, Eva."

"That's nice to know…" Once I realized that my dad was never coming back for me, the hate for both of my parents slowly grew, the longer I stayed. My dad is the only one I should hate. "Is there any way I could get to her?"

"Yes, but we're going to have to camouflage you with the uniform jumpsuit and sneak you in… and change your hair colour."

"I'm down for that," I answer.

"We can start now. I have a bunch of hair dye in my room. Pick a colour."

Leilani Gracetta

When Cheyenne finishes dying my hair—I chose purple—she gives me one of her uniforms that covers all of my tattoos. We collect everything and go out to Hunter's car. But before we take off, Rholanda hands me her old bureaucratic uniform, "Take this, and my pass card. Don't make eye contact with anyone in the Chancellery."

"I'll try."

"Neither of you have training today?" I ask.

"Not when the entire municipality is on lockdown because of you. A lot of us are happy we finally get to be home, so thanks for being on the loose, Eva."

"You're welcome…" I murmur. Being put on the spot isn't as fun as it seems. We go to the base first. Cheyenne gets out first and runs to the front of the building to check if any of the doors are open, seemingly not, then she rushes around to the back. It takes a bit of time for her to return. "Some of them are there, but she's not."

Tokyo Narita

"I'm pretty sure she still lives in the same house," Hunter says. "We can try there, see if she's home."

"Try that," Cheyenne replies as she puts her seatbelt back on.

She still lives where everything fucking started? I'm not angry at it, but what the fuck? Rholanda isn't even in the same house she lived in while she was an aristocrat and before she had Cheyenne. But I guess it's up to individual circumstances… and if it's her choice, then okay.

It fucks me up, being back here. I was six and happy, the last time I was here. Now I'm 23 and got half of my memory beaten the fuck out of me, so I barely remember much from that time anymore. "Hi, mom." I smile or at least try to make out a smile with my lips before she quickly pulls me into a firm hug. I wish I could physically see how she looks, instead of a shadow.

"Eva… I'm sorry…"

Leilani Gracetta

For a moment, the pain and hate melt away, and I close my eyes, shedding a couple of tears. "It's his fault," Since he disowned me and left mom's life, I'm sure in shambles, I'm not even gonna call the fucker dad anymore, "and I'm gonna kill him. But we need your help."

"With what?"

"We're going to sneak into the Chancellery, we're going against the dictator. We might need more than just two soldiers. Rholanda gave me her old uniform. Think you can gather an army for us… lieutenant?"

"I…I'll see what I can do."

"Thank you, mom."

"Long day…"

"Tomorrow will be an even longer day."

Tokyo Narita

"That's if we get caught."

"True…" I respond before rubbing my eyes.

"Goodnight, Cheyenne."

"Goodnight."

Since Cheyenne is on the couch, I have to sleep with Hunter this time. I crawl into his bed next to him, then close my eyes. And just as I'm drifting off, I feel his arm wrap around me.

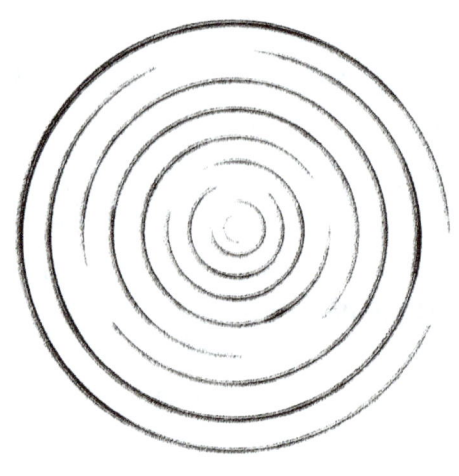

CHAPTER 3

"Meet you there." I smile before getting out of Hunter's car. It took a bit of time, but we all eventually agreed to me hopping the borders, while he and Cheyenne go through the checkpoints and walk or run to the centre ring. We're only five rings away.

When I get there a little earlier than them, I immediately know which high rise building the dictator resides in. There are five buildings for the five ringed districts. And he's obviously in the tallest one, where he can see over all of the borders.

I wait for Hunter and Cheyenne. When they finally get past the checkpoint and see me, we enter into the building. Now, I can only assume with the number of shadows in front of me. It's likely bureaucrats, aristocrats, and soldiers ambling about the main floor of the Chancellery as if daylight is still sprawling through the windows. No one pays even slight attention to us, well, until Cheyenne half way waves at someone nearby. "Who?"

Tokyo Narita

"It's my dad…" She whispers loudly.

Rholanda's husband, Cole. I forgot he was an officer.

"Elevator or stairs?" Hunter asks.

"We're not climbing up all those flights of stairs, we're on a time limit. Fuck that, take the elevator."

"Yes, ma'am."

Soon joined by Cole, when we make it up to the top floor, he points out to us where the dictator's bureau is. "Is he in there?"

"He left almost an hour ago. But be quick just in case he's not gone for long."

"Thanks, Cole."

Hunter goes first, pushing down on the door handle to see if the door is unlocked; it arches down. So he opens the door, only halfway, to see if the room is empty. "Noah?"

"Oh shit…" I hear Cheyenne curse under her breath.

Noah Victor, his son. The last time I've seen him, his father was scolding me for something, and he had a look of dismay on his face. But not at me, at the dictator. I don't think he likes his dad very much, and he has many reasons why. One revolves around an alleged rumour that the dictator used to beat his mother.

Allegedly because neither Noah or his mother confirmed or denied it after a divorce.

"Okay, uh…" Hunter falters, "do you know where your father is? Do you know when he's coming back?"

"He left an hour ago. I don't know, he left me here."

"Could you go… distract him for us when he comes back?"

He doesn't answer, but we get him out of the bureau anyway. And after Cheyenne shuts and locks the door after him, she creates a bright orange, transparent layer over the door, shielding it from being opened with… her powers?

"You have powers too?"

"Yes."

I shake my head. "Okay. I'll ask you later." We start fucking shit up, ripping and burning documents and folders from his desk and destroying his other shit. "His desktop is still on." I laugh after accidentally smashing my elbow on the keyboard. "Let's make a fucking announcement! Help me, Hunter." I've always wondered how he's able to appear on the screens of different devices from here. "Is it on?" I ask while grinning.

"Now, it is."

"Good morning, Tokyo Narita, it's Eva Vega. Nolan isn't here right now." I laugh. "So, in the absence of him, I ORDER YOU FUCKERS TO RELEASE ALL OF THE DIVIDED CITIZENS!" I assert before giving the desk a loud and stern bang with my fist. "I SAID NOW!" I shove the desktop back, making it crash onto the floor in front of the desk.

"We're so dead."

"If he can fucking catch us!"

"Shit! That quick!" Cheyenne gasps as we all begin to hear heavy kicks from behind the door. "It's him."

"Open the door," I say as Hunter quickly uses a chair to break a window.

"Are you sure, Eva?"

"FUCK IT! OPEN THE DOOR!"

"FUCK YOU, DICTATOR DICKHEAD!" I cackle as soon as Cheyenne lets the shield deteriorate, he finally kicks the door in, and we all dart out from the broken window.

◎◎◎◎◎◎◎◎◎

We're not done with him yet. He just doesn't know when our next strike will be, and now that we destroyed most of his essential shit, he won't be able to make demands to his puppets.

Nothing has ever felt more fucking freeing. I'm actually hyped now. "When are we going to make the next power trip?"

"I would wait a couple of days, to keep the officers off of our asses."

I shrug, "Okay."

"And I still have to go get my car."

"Oh yeah… when?"

"I'll go later tonight."

"Eva, Hunter," We hear Cheyenne call after opening the backdoor, "mom needs to talk to you."

"What's up?"

"Did you destroy his office?" She asks, sounding a bit concerned.

"Yeah, we fucking did!" I laugh. "But it's not the only thing we're going to do."

"I like your plan, Eva, but you did not hit the nail. You didn't really do much yet. What happened?"

"We snuck into the Chancellery, Cole showed us where his office was. Noah was in there. So we got him out and fucked all his shit up… and made a special announcement."

"I saw, but did you try to find out where his other places are, though?"

"What other places?!"

"Eva, you didn't go through his computer?"

"No! I fucking destroyed it, and all the documents."

"You're supposed to look for useful information before destroying it."

"I'm sorry. We didn't have enough time. What are these places you're talking about?"

"I don't know if it's the same now, but the last time I looked at the blueprint before leaving, he wanted to build something like a lab underground. I don't know where it is, but I'm certain that he followed through with it since he followed through with everything else that were once secrets."

"An underground lab? What the fuck?"

"You heard me."

"Damn it!" Not only that, but we also don't know who to ask about this underground lab. "Why didn't you tell us that beforehand?"

"I thought you were going to look through the computer and find out about it. But now, you know."

Leilani Gracetta

"Eva…"

"Hm?"

"I have to get my car."

"Okay…" I answer before lazily rolling to the other side of the bed. "Can I go with you?"

"It might be too dangerous for you, Eva."

"I don't care. Dangerous is my prison name."

He sighs, "Fine. Come on."

I'm still a fugitive, I didn't forget. Just because we destroyed most of the dictator's important documents doesn't mean his real followers won't continue to work under his laws. And that means I'm still wanted for possible execution. We bolt a beeline from the North district to the centre district. As we near the last five rings, we notice more soldiers are guarding the checkpoints. I watch Hunter dash up the last wall first, then I come from behind a tree believing that the area in front of me is clear, ready to dash up the wall myself.

Until I crash into something heavy in the darkness, in front of me. "Shit!"

"Eva," I hear Hunter call from above, "are you okay?"

"Yeah!" I say as I pick myself back up. The beaming light of a flashlight shines in front of me, and a voice, a guy's voice, speaks. "Eva?"

"Oh, shit, no…" I curse under my breath. I know that voice. "Ivan!"

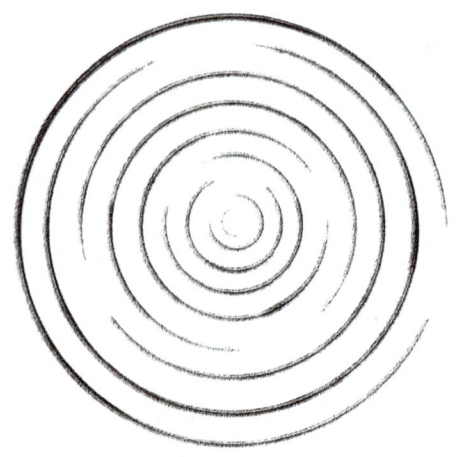

CHAPTER 4

"Did we just run into Ivan Andrade?" I ask rhetorically.

"We did," Hunter replies.

"How? Fucking how…?" I'm pretty fucking sure me blowing a gaping hole into his chest killed him. I watched him struggle, then stop moving before fleeing. "We need to tell Rholanda because… I'm not sure… I don't know anymore, Hunter."

"I'm concerned with why he let you go."

"That's not what he'd normally do. That's not the Ivan I knew. And why is he patrolling the borders? He's the fucking aristocrat."

"Let's ask Rholanda in the morning."

"Look, we're sorry. We left to go get Hunter's car in the middle of the night. We ran into him, patrolling the border, and we're trying to figure out how he's still alive after I swear I killed the asshole. And for some reason, he let me go, which is not usual from him."

"First of all, Eva, you know you're still wanted. Hunter, you get your ass caught, you know what's going to happen. Both of you are hardheaded. Y'all need to get that together before both of you get thrown in front of the dictator. If Ivan decides to report that he spotted you, we're all fucked, keep that in mind."

"We know."

"But since he already knows you're out and running around, I would wait a bit to see if he is going to report it. If he doesn't, this is a good opportunity to ask him about that lab we talked about yesterday. If he'll tell you anything."

"Damn, you're right about that, Rholanda."

"But I said wait. Please, wait. Don't go out there immediately."

"Okay, we won't." I smile. I'm not smiling because we're planning on disobeying her, but because we're not her children, yet she cares for us like we are.

"We'll be here for a while," Hunter says as we head up the stairs, "anything you want to do?"

"Actually…" I quickly open the door to Cheyenne's room, hearing her snoring, sound asleep. "Yes."

"What?"

As soon as he turns towards me, I wrap my arms around his neck and kiss him on the lips. He rather quickly perceives the hint, resting his hands on the sides of my body below my shirt. He pushes his entire weight against mine, and we both fall back onto the bed.

After we wait for a little more than two days—and nothing has happened—assuming he hasn't reported us, I go with

Hunter and Cheyenne to approach Ivan. They walk up to him first while I hide behind a nearby tree, listening in. And just when I think I will eventually have to approach him to get an answer out of him, I hear them walking back, then Hunter grabs onto my wrist. "It's in the mountains." He says.

"Which one?" Should've guessed that one correctly since nobody lives in the mountains. Except for the central district, which is built into where the two ranges intersect. "Can we ask mom?"

"She may not know. Even though the lieutenants are the powers over us soldiers and we have the hidden places memorized, he has more power than them. I don't think he tells them everything because if we don't know, they most likely don't either. But we can ask her, in case she does know."

"Let's go." Now that I think about it, it's weird how Ivan just flat out told them something that's supposed to be a secret. I'm pretty sure he's still the aristocrat since he's somehow still alive. So, as we're hopping the borders going towards East Narita, Cheyenne abruptly stops while standing atop one of the walls.

"What is it?" I ask loudly from below.

She eventually comes down. "The dictator."

"Where?"

"I know you can't see this, Eva, but you know how you made that announcement, and everybody saw you? Well, it's one of those."

"I destroyed the desktop."

"Not this one."

Which confirms our suspicion, there is another place. "Fuck it, that confirms that we're on the right path. Let's just ask and try to find it where Ivan said it is." When we get to my mom's, we quickly ask her the question, that we immediately figure she doesn't know the answer to. But she offers to help if we need it, in which we gladly accept. Then we go back to inform Rholanda, who is in the kitchen with Cheyenne's dad. Just in time because we might just need Cole for this.

"Wait," Rholanda asks, "you actually trust what Ivan told you? And he's apparently on border patrol now?"

"It doesn't sound like the old, pro-Victor Ivan, and it's a huge downgrade," I laugh, "but yes."

"This sounds like an obvious trap when Ivan is telling you things. But if you want to follow through with it, be careful. If this isn't a trap and he was honest, let me know when you find the lab."

"Yes, ma'am." I nod, before Hunter, Cheyenne, and I rush up the stairs to change into our jumpsuits.

"What are we looking for, exactly?"

"Don't know yet, but if it's in either range, then we have to search both of them for it. If we don't already find it here."

"Okay." We begin to follow Cheyenne with her GPS on her phone. And it takes at least a few hours for us to run through the entire range, avoiding obstacles, eventually finding nothing, yet. "It has to be in the other one. He better not be shitting us. I'll blow another hole into his chest." We quickly switch to the other mountain range. After following Cheyenne for a couple more hours, we inevitably find where a part of the land collapses, far into the mountain, like it's been built into. Cheyenne immediately pinpoints our location on the map to Rholanda.

"He definitely wasn't shitting us," Cheyenne affirms, "this isn't shown on the map."

"We gotta go after the dictator this time. We can't have this fucker walking around again, who knows what other places he has."

"That's true. But first, how do we get in?" Hunter asks.

"Good question."

"Looks like there's a path to a tunnel down there. Maybe we could go through there…"

Tokyo Narita

"Good eyes, Cheyenne."

"Thank you."

So we walk down this weird and dark tunnel, and it takes a bit of time for us to get to what we're looking for, far into it.

"Oh my God…" We both hear Cheyenne whisper loudly before running forward. "It's right here… well, down there." She states while looking down at a bright light coming up from a vent in the concrete.

"How are we going to get down there without getting caught."

"We're not going down there from here. But if it's under this tunnel, then that means if we go further down here…"

When we get to the end of the tunnel, and we're in a building some number of feet below the ground, we split up. Cheyenne goes her own way, and I follow Hunter. The lights are beaming, and the place is not

34

entirely vacant, as I can tell by the number of voices and shadows around us. "He better be here."

"What is this supposed to be? This is the only door with a caution sign on it." Hunter asks as he pushes down the door handle. "Ahhh, shit!"

"What is it?"

He doesn't answer for at least a full minute. "Okay, Eva… what can you see?" He immediately asks, sounding disturbed.

"I don't know, not much, blue light… and tall shadows. You tell me what you see."

"There's fucking bodies in large tanks of water."

"WHAT?!"

"There are bodies in individual tanks!"

"Are they dead?"

"They're not moving, and they have electrode wires attached to their heads. Where'd all of these bodies come from?"

"How many are there?"

"Too many. It's like… half of the population is here. Even children."

Did he just say…? If there's that many, then it is half the population! The population I'm grouped into! "Hunter… this is half the population."

"How do you know?"

"Remember, I told you they throw us into camps to let the soldiers kill us?" If I'm right, "These are the people they killed so far. Believe me now?"

"There's Ivan's body… but where's the hole you burned into his chest?"

"IVAN? WHERE?"

"Right —" He's only able to get one word out before we feel hands snatch us from the top of our heads, then slam the sides of our heads into each other. "Oh shit…" I mumble under my breath after opening my eyes to a tall shadow standing where we were just standing.

"I was just getting ready to shove both of you into these."

The dictator. "You're not shoving either of us into shit! What other fucked up things are you doing that I need to let the citizens know?!" I wouldn't be surprised if he's secretly trying to annihilate the entire population by the time he chooses to stop being the dictator. But he wouldn't kill his privileged babies.

"None of your business and they're not going to know anything. I know you're only here because of Ivan. I wanted him to tell you."

"No, we're here because of Rholanda. We only needed Ivan to tell us where this is." I laugh.

"Behind you," Hunter chuckles.

He stays silent for a second, trying to comprehend why we're laughing at him until Cheyenne runs up and tackles him from behind. Or at least we think she has him at first. "Where'd he go?!" She exclaims.

And again, Hunter and I immediately get our heads slammed together, from behind. "Will you fucking STOP THAT!"

"You have them too?"

Now that we know we don't have a bionic advantage over him, it's still three of us against him. "TACKLE HIM!" I demand before dashing to the further side of the room. I let out a cackle as he at first lunges forward, attempting to snatch me, thinking I was going to attack him first.

I perch myself atop a tank, watching as three shadows brawl with each other. Cheyenne eventually pulls a smart move and tugs out what might be an elastic band holding his man-bun in place, impairing his vision. And when they get him to run out of energy tricking him with their strategy, they hold him up for me. "COME GET HIM, EVA!"

Leilani Gracetta

I was lucky enough to escape. But there are thousands of innocent people like me, like all of us, still stuck and suffering, and hundreds who couldn't pull through all of the abuse and lost their fight to live. All because of this fucker, excuse me, or cipher—is holding a grudge against his stepmother. It was wrong of her to assassinate his father, I understand, but it's evil to take it out on us.

For this to never happen again, I have to do this. I approach him, gathering all of my energy into my left hand. I push my hand into his chest, letting my energy blow a gaping hole through his back.

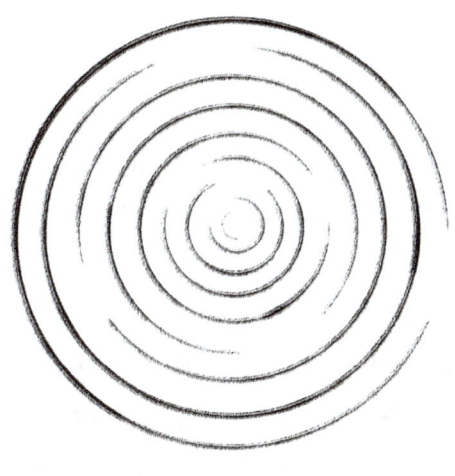

CHAPTER 5

"I don't want to be a dictator, Eva," Noah says, "watching my father be an asshole all these years. It's too much responsibility, I can't trust myself with it. Maybe one of you can take it…"

Ivan or Noah is legally supposed to take it since he's now dead. But since both of them refuse to accept the offer now, it has to be one of us. We all turn our heads in Rholanda's and mom's direction.

Rholanda immediately notices, "Nope. I was the aristocrat for too long. I'm done being involved."

"Sorry, sweetie," Mom answers, "I love my job. Nope."

"I can't trust myself either. Not with dictatorship." Cheyenne takes a step back.

"I'll do it." Someone finally steps forward. Hunter.

"Are you sure, Hunter? It's a hell of a job."

"Sure. We can start this over, by releasing the divided half of the population and destroying that segregation law."

I wrap my arms around his neck before kissing him on the lips. "I love that plan, you cipher." I chuckle, "I love you."

"I love you too, cipher."

Acknowledgements

In loving memory of Christina, Emily, Charlie, and my grandmother.

Thank you, Landon and Kantessa, for staying by my side and believing in me. I love you.